4 SHORT ROMANCE STORIES COLLECTION #3 COPY

Easy to Read - a Large Print, Short Paragraphs, with Clean or Sweet, Some Instalove and Feel-Good atmosphere of Short Stories

Misha Quinn

CONTENTS

BONUS CONTENT FOR YOU

Get the FREE bonus prologue to the 2nd book in The Salamander series when you sign up for my newsletter:

http://www.mishaquinn.com/

Please subscribe to the newsletter and download Misha Quinn bonus content.

Sincerely yours, Misha Quinn

EDELWEISS FOR PROM QUEEN

Olivia was looking forward to her high school's prom. Everything that had happened before had foreshadowed events that promised to make it extraordinary. This suspicion had not left the girl for days. She knew that today would be the beginning of her new life - the life of an adult girl, and that school would be in the past. And what this new adult life of hers would be was entirely up to her, Olivia.

The mountains, with their pointed snowy peaks that pierced the sky, towered around the town where she lived, like the teeth of a dragon opening its mouth to catch its prey. Some mountains were shrouded in clouds that never seemed to fly from there. Other peaks were lower, and the snow did not cover them year-round. They were just as sharp as their more prominent companions. The mountains were a favorite view that Olivia was always admiring in all weathers.

The girl remembered how, a week before prom night, Emma, the acclaimed beauty of their graduating class and perhaps the entire school, had announced a contest to see how she would choose her prom date.

As usual in pleasant summer weather, the pupils in their class were spending their recess time between classes sitting in the schoolyard. Emma sat on the back of a bench, placing her beautiful, slender legs on its seat. The girl wore miniskirts if the school still allowed her and took every opportunity to show off her legs in the most helpful way.

Girls and boys surrounded Emma alike. Spending time between classes in the company of Emma was prestigious because she chose her "entourage" carefully.

Emma's companions and companions could be called nothing but an "entourage." Everyone had a role to play. Emma's entourage helped her do her homework, some taught her how to use the computer, and some shaded her beauty. Yes, shadowing Emma's beauty was also the job of some girls who valued themselves so little that they wanted to stand out, at least by basking in the glow of this beauty. And who shaded her beauty, Emma selected her "entourage" with special partiality.

Guys who were not in Emma's "entourage" also competed to get the attention of the recognized beauty of their school. But so far, no one had made her their permanent girlfriend. Perhaps that goal was entirely unattainable for them, for Emma had so far been interested only in her success, not in the feelings "subjects" might have for her.

Olivia, who was sitting at recess that day near the bench where Emma and her "entourage" were seated, saw Emma throwing her beautiful blond hair back from her shoulders in a circle of admirers of her beauty that included both boys and girls, but necessarily girls who could not match her beauty, declare in a whimsical tone:

"I want an Edelweiss on my dress. Whoever brings me an Edelweiss for prom night will dance the Prom Queen dance with me in front of everyone."

Everyone fell silent. Emma's confidence that she would be Prom Queen was not in question. But the boys knew how hard it was to find Edelweiss in their mountains. It is only possible for those who can hike high in the mountains and know the places where this flower can bloom.

Emma continued.

"And besides, I promise my kiss to this daredevil."

The surrounding boys just opened their mouths in amazement. Wow, Emma-the one who did not let anyone else do anything-or, at least, everyone thought she did-was going to kiss the lucky guy who would bring her the Edelweiss! Unheard of.

Sitting away from Emma and her entourage, Olivia heard what Ella had said. Olivia glanced skeptically at the future Prom Queen. The girl knew she could not compete with Emma in popularity, but the way Emma manipulated the guys who looked up to her and the way

Emma treated her so-called "girlfriends" often made Olivia angry.

Olivia was an excellent student, but she never sought recognition for her looks, which were the most ordinary. But something in her soul told her that intelligence did not prevent outward attractiveness.

However, this aspect of life would have to be dealt with as carefully as Olivia dealt with her studies. But for now, the girl had no desire to do so. That is why a heightened sense of fairness and simple female competition pushed Olivia to compete with Emma at the prom. Not expecting anything good from her venture, she accepted the rules of the game of beauty and will sacrifice the habits of "her boyfriend" for it.

Olivia ordered the best prom dress she could find, made at a local atelier. The girl also tried to put on fancy makeup and asked her older sister to help her do it.

Word of Emma's impossible condition quickly spread throughout the school. Even students from classes two years younger than her graduating class were talking about her demand. One guy in their senior class, Noah, had also heard about Emma's condition. However, Noah did not need to bring girls flowers to win their attention. Girls will forgive him anything for his attention, even the fact that he was not any gentleman.

In Emma's case, however, he was attracted because he competed with other guys for the prize.

Noah, who had heard about the contest announced by Emma, solved the problem. He was the most popular guy at their school, and they felt only he should be Emma's prom date. Not that Noah liked her very much. Noah did not want a girl like himself, as his date, with big ambitions and high expectations of the surrounding people.

Noah was quite comfortable being a handsome man who was an excellent American soccer player and not good at school. Still, he was sure that with his good looks and success in sports, he would get into a prestigious college without high academic performance. Besides, Noah was a rock climber and knew places where Edelweiss could grow.

When Emma mentioned her requirement for a companion at graduation, many in her entourage thought only Noah could bring her Edelweiss. Perhaps Emma had created such an assignment, impossible for many other guys. Everyone knew she was "pining" for Noah, who did not give her enough attention, preferring the company of less demanding girls who just adored him.

Emma wanted Noah, the most popular boy in their school, in her "entourage," but that had not happened.

Olivia did not know that Noah decided he needed to stand out from the crowd in another way and be Emma's prom partner. However, the day before prom, Olivia saw Noah haggling for a bouquet of Edelweiss with one of the Highlanders who brought flowers, honey, and crafts from their village to the market in their town, in a valley between the mountains.

The girl realized this guy did not bother to go to the mountains for Emma but bought a bouquet spectacularly handed this bouquet of Edelweiss to Emma, just melted with pleasure; Olivia knew she would tell no one about this incident in the market. But a sense of injustice had settled in her soul that had to be corrected.

She did not know what to do but was determined to set the record straight and restore justice. And that was the reason for her worries: the same day, Olivia saw another boy from their class, the inconspicuous Liam, also brought an Edelweiss flower to Emma.

Liam's hands were bloodied, and he was limping a little, which told her he had climbed the mountains and found the Edelweiss flower for Emma himself. But Emma, who was carefully cradling the bouquet of Edelweiss given to her by Noah, carelessly accepted the lonely flower and immediately put it on the table, forgetting about it. She was fascinated with her new admirer - Noah, and his bouquet of Edelweiss flowers she pinned on her dress.

Defeated in the struggle for the heart of the acknowledged beauty, Liam stepped aside and soon left this classmate meeting unnoticed.

Olivia took a lonely Edelweiss flower lying on the table, twirled it in her hands, squeezed it in her hands, and pressed it to her heart. The girl thought of how much willpower this puny pupil, completely invisible in their class, must have had to do what the girl of his dreams, Emma, wanted him to do. He went to the mountains and got that flower; this Emma did not appreciate his act, preferring the handsome Noah, who did not even dust his boots in search of Edelweiss for her.

Long before prom night, Olivia had turned her attention to Liam. They had nothing in common except that they were in the same class. One day, he helped her with her homework without asking for anything. The guy just wanted to help her, that's all.

And then Olivia suddenly noticed Liam's eyes were attentive and kind behind his large diopter glasses. The guy's hands were wiry, and he seemed capable of lifting the entire globe with little effort if necessary. Olivia learned Liam practiced karate from her chess partner, which she was passionate about. Still, no one knew about it except for a tight circle of his friends.

Olivia was increasingly interested in him, Liam, and not Noah. The girl felt in her heart that the competition announced by Emma for her prom date was the wrong move.

It was time for the prom. Olivia's classmates were grooming themselves for the day as if the rest of their lives depended on it. Though it was the opposite, the prom ended their high school life and began a new adult life in college and work. Olivia was keeping up with them, but she had another crucial thing on her schedule for that day.

On the morning of prom day, a knock was on the door of Liam's house. He opened the door himself and was surprised to see Olivia, his classmate, on the doorstep.

Olivia was dressed in a simple tank top and denim shorts, and her dark hair was braided into two pigtails. She looked more like a kindergarten girl than a senior in high school. She did not look like she was going to prom like the other girls in her class.

The girl stood in front of Liam, a little embarrassed, but the determined expression on her face said that her cause was very important.

"I heard you do not want to go to the prom," she said, rocking from heel to toe.

Liam nodded silently, not wanting to talk about the subject.

Olivia continued for him.

"Alone... You do not want to go there alone, do you?"

Liam raised his eyebrows in surprise and nodded silently once more. He did not understand what this Olivia, who was doing well in her life, wanted. At least she was not humiliated, as Emma humiliated him in front of all their classmates.

But the girl continued. "Will you come with me?"

Liam looked at her dazedly. "Olivia, why does she need me to go with her," he thought, but at the exact moment, he answered.

"Yes, of course!"

Both were embarrassed. But the deed was done; the arrangement was made.

Olivia spun on the spot, waved at him, and, running away, shouted cheerfully,

"Well, call me an hour before prom, and come get me!"

Liam was left standing in the doorway of his house, completely dumbfounded. But a warm feeling was spreading in his chest that this girl remembered him and that someone still wanted to see him as a prom date, despite his failure with the Edelweiss flower for Emma.

When it was time to go to the prom, Liam took his father's car and drove it to pick up Olivia. When he drove up to her house, a girl appeared on the doorstep in such a gorgeous dress with her hair so beautifully styled that Liam initially thought it was not her but some friend of hers. But it was Olivia. Her mother and older sister helped her create an image of a princess who wore little makeup and did not suit her usual boyish dress.

But what struck Liam the most was that an Edelweiss flower was attached to the corset of Olivia's beautiful dress. Somehow Liam knew it was his flower, the one he had brought to Emma, which she had rejected by tossing carelessly onto the table behind her.

Liam felt his cheeks turn pink with pleasure. He realized Olivia was doing something unusual for him. But the boy did not understand why - after all, he had brought this flower for Emma...

While Liam wondered why Olivia had chosen his flower to decorate her prom dress, the girl, carefully picking up the flaps of the crinoline of a pink dress like "Princess," went down the steps of the house to Liam's car. Surprised, the boy did not realize that he had to open the car door for her and still stood by the door of Olivia's house.

When Liam sprinted from his seat and ran up to the car to open Olivia's door, they almost collided and had to put their hands on the hood to avoid falling over.

The girl was not the least bit embarrassed by this, and she laughed mischievously. Olivia could see that she had thrown Liam into a stupor, which made her laugh. And she was also amused that she would do something good for him - a quiet and inconspicuous but strong-minded guy who would be a worthy friend to any girl who would understand what she needed from a life partner - loyalty and reliability.

Then she and Olivia laughed merrily as they tried to shove her crinoline into the car and close the door so the dress's fabric would not be damaged. The lavish crinoline kept trying to stick out of the car, taking up almost all the space in its small interior and looking like pink sea foam that had somehow miraculously ended up in an old sports car with an open top.

When the young people finally got into the car and folded the crinoline of Olivia's dress so that Liam could drive, they drove carefully to the school, in whose hall the prom was being held.

The hall where the school held the prom was already full of graduates. Like birds of paradise, pairs of yesterday's schoolboys and schoolgirls fluttered about on the boardwalk. They all looked very unfamiliar now-almost like adults. The outfits that almost no one had ever worn at a party until now suddenly stressed the attractiveness of the freshly shining girls and the suddenly mature boys.

Girls who had been mere schoolgirls yesterday were now fairy-tale beauties with a trail of expensive perfume behind them, most likely from their mothers and older sisters. The guys, who suddenly all looked like dandies, were awkwardly adjusting the cuffs of their white starched shirts and bow ties, which they were not used to.

The music was playing, and the DJ was trying to keep everyone entertained.

While the graduates were talking and some were dancing to soft music selected by the DJ, especially for this formal part of the evening, everyone was given pieces of paper with the names of the candidates for Prom Queen. When everyone was ready to choose one girl as a Prom Queen, the papers were collected, and votes were counted.

When it was time to announce the Prom Queen, everyone froze. In principle, no one expected anything new from the secret ballot because everyone's known favorite was here - Emma. The girl was dazzlingly beautiful in a light, glittery dress that fit her body like a glove and a tiara she wore beforehand. But this predictability of the voting results left many wishing something unusual would happen. The condition Emma had set for her companion hurt everyone.

And Olivia was not the only one who appreciated what Liam had done for Emma. The other girls also noticed that this guy was worth more attention than the haughty, handsome Noah, who did not pay any attention to his companions, but, on the contrary, demanded to show their adoration for his person.

And a miracle happened. After the vote count, the evening's host, one of last year's graduates and former Prom Queen, announced into the microphone,

"And now congratulations - the Prom Queen is chosen... Olivia!"

The host added Olivia's last name, but everyone knew who she was. Olivia went up to the platform, leading Liam by the hand. Surprised by this turn of events, they stood there and received congratulations from the host and applause from their friends and prom attendees.

Only one couple was not happy about it-the best couple in school-at least until this evening. Emma and Noah stood on the side-lines, unable to understand. They saw every-thing had been so rightly calculated. They were, without a doubt, the most beautiful couple of the evening, but somehow, they did not get enough votes to give Emma the long-desired title of Prom Queen.

Besides, Emma did not seem as attractive to Noah now as she had just a moment ago. Turning away from Emma, he looked at Olivia and tried to figure out why he had not noticed her.

But Olivia was not looking toward Emma and Noah. Her eyes were fixed on Liam, who kept his eyes on her. He proudly held out his hand and led her into the slow dance of the Prom Queen.

The couple was spinning to a romantic tune the DJ had set up for them.

Olivia looked into Liam's eyes, and gradually, their faces were so close together that their lips touched. A light kiss, a gentle embrace, was the beginning of their budding first love. Now there were only the two of them and their budding love.

The End

Copyright by Misha Quinn, June 2023

DALIA AND THE MODERN SUBWAY KNIGHT

At the very rush hour, Dalia made her way to the passageway gates of the subway station in the heart of the vast metropolis.

Every day, the subway was her way of getting around the vast city. The girl was not at all afraid of the subway. In it, she only had to know the basic rules of conduct, and then it was possible to use it safely enough.

For example? A young girl should be able to ride the subway in the late evening hours. Or get on the first or last car of a subway train. There are many other things you should not have to talk about - knowing clearly that there is nothing of value in the backpack hanging from your shoulder on one strap. Or remember to clasp your purse with valuables such as your passport, cell phone, wallet, and keys in the crowd walking inside the subway crossing from station to station. And in public places in the metropolis, it's best to keep your purse in front of you and never lean it back.

Dalia was rushing to the institute for a math course on this day. The girl was in the exact sciences and had recently enrolled in the best university in the country for applied mathematics, which she was very proud of.

Dalia's appearance was ordinary - at least, that is what the girl thought. Her roots were in Asia, which meant that traditionally, her ties to her family were significant and robust. Her dark hair was always neatly braided into two thick braids. Dalia could not see well and wore glasses for her near vision. These glasses spoiled her, but the girl was not embarrassed by that. She did not want to wear lenses - they irritated her eyes. Dalia had not thought about correcting her eyesight in other ways yet.

Dahlia, passionate about science or her future in science, was not interested in boyfriends or romance. Her classmates nick-named her "our rosebud" because her appearance was as fresh and unpretentious as an unopened rosebud. Everything about the girl only promised a future flowering of beauty and awareness of her attractiveness.

In the meantime, Dalia walked down the long underpass passage to the subway station, where her daily commute to the university began.

The girl stopped at the line drawn on the platform for the train to stop. No closer than one meter to the edge of the platform was recommended. From the dark tunnel, increasingly intensified, first blew a stream of air, fished out in the darkness of the subway train's run in front of her, and then the noise of the train was heard.

Here the headlights of the first car of the subway train appeared. Dalia, clutching her purse tighter, looked for where the second carriage of the train would stop so as not to lose a second and slip into it first. There was a crowd around her, and everyone was thinking about the same thing - how to get into the carriage and take one of the few empty seats along the carriage walls.

Dalia deftly slipped inside the carriage but realized the crowd had pinned her against the carriage wall opposite the front doors. The girl did not want to stand there, but there was nowhere to go. Now it was better not to move and elbow her way to a place where no one else would approach.

The girl settled against the wall of the carriage.

The train moved and pulled noisily into the subway tunnel in a few seconds.

More passengers piled into the carriage at the next station, and the situation at the wall, against which the girl now found herself specifically pressed, was not as good as it had been five minutes ago. Dalia could hardly breathe.

On the one hand, some man, constantly squinting at the girl and trying to mutter an apology, had his back on her. Still, he could do nothing about it - he was just as pinned down and almost flattened by the other passengers. On the other side, a middle-aged lady found herself pressed against her, sighing noisily, turning her head, and secretly trying to push Dalia away from her and take her place.

Dalia suddenly felt dizzy. It was stuffy in the carriage, and perhaps the girl had not had a good breakfast before she left home, which was now obviously bad for her well-being.

Dalia closed her eyes in exhaustion. She was tired of elbowing away at the backs and sides of the passengers, squeezing her. Her ears were buzzing, and she saw a flicker of light lines and dots in her closed eyes.

"Am I going to faint?" she thought and felt nothing except that she had nowhere to fall, so tightly squeezed.

"And what happens when I pass out?" she thought. She had already imagined the picture of slipping to the subway car floor and a crowd of passengers gathering around her, staring at her injured in the crash.

The picture gave her strength. She put her hands before her and pressed them against the guy's chest. Her face hardened with effort and turned pale. Dalia was no longer thinking about who was looking at her. She was just afraid of passing out here. The girl had almost resigned herself to the fact that she was about to fall to the floor of this subway car. Or rather, now she would collapse, squeezed by these people. She falls silently to the vehicle's floor at the next station when they leave the subway carriage.

Dalia suddenly felt the circle of bodies squeezing her loose expand at that moment. The girl opened her eyes and saw right in front of her the same guy with whom, a minute ago, she had been pressing her hands to find a little space to breathe.

By some miracle, this short but sturdy guy had created some passenger-free space around her.

The guy did not yell to those around him: "Make room; she's going to be sick!"

He just acted. His arms formed an archway where Dalia felt free enough to breathe and regain her ability to cope with the situation.

The guy held back the pressure of the passengers' bodies for several minutes. The muscles in his arms swelled with tension, and his face flushed, but he did not give up. His persistence paid off-the girl's face turned pink again, and she could breathe.

Dalia could not yet speak to thank her savior, but she suddenly felt the need to show her gratitude to him in another way.

The girl touched her palm to the lad's cheek lightly, like a whiff of wind, and immediately pulled it away. It was not her rule to show something like that to men. It was not customary in their family. She could thank her father or younger brother that way, not a strange guy in a subway car. But Dalia could not help herself!

Her protector did not understand what had happened at first and then blushed with embarrassment. He had not expected such a reaction from this girl, who seemed so timid.

The guy smiled and, without lowering his arms, still protecting Dalia from the crowd of people, said, looking Dalia in the eyes,

"You are welcome. I just had to do it."

The girl could finally utter,

"Thank you... Without your help, I would have fallen... No one but you understood that."

The guy might have nodded and looked around, and said,

"Well, everything will be all right now. Here is the station at last. They will all come out now; I know it. I ride this branch of the subway line every day."

Dalia replied in surprise.

"And so do I...no, I do not have to get off at this station yet. It is just that I ride here every day, too."

There was surprise and joy in the girl's voice. The joy that she and her savior had something in common-the same route in the morning and perhaps in the evening.

But suddenly, it occurred to the girl that she had not even asked her savior's name. Dalia timidly asked,

"What is your name?"

The guy replied,

"Amir."

As the crowd of passengers streamed out of the carriage onto the station platform, the girl replied,

"And my name is Dalia. And I am a university student."

The guy stared at her in surprise.

"Dalia..." he said, staring at her. "You do not remember me at all, do you?"

The girl sensed some trick in his question and froze, not daring to admit she did not understand who was before her.

Amir continued,

"You and I are in the same class at this university. And you did not even notice me. And I noticed you there a long time ago..."

His voice lowered as if he were confessing something terrible. Yes, looking at this girl and not knowing how to start a conversation was not very good.

Dalia looked dazedly at Amir. What a shame! They were in the same class, sitting in the same lectures, and she did not remember him.

Of course, there were more than a hundred people in their course. The same lectures were for all the students in a huge classroom, where it was impossible to remember anyone except those who sat next to them. Classes on separately chosen subjects of study were held in small groups. Apparently, Dalia had not been in such courses with Amir until now. She certainly would have remembered him if they had been in the same small group.

What a shame! Why did he notice her, even in the big classroom, and she did not see him?

Amir seemed to read all her feelings on her face-so. It was changing. The boy hurried to reassure the troubled girl.

"It is okay. I understand everything. Unfortunately, we have not shared a small group class, so you do not remember me. Of course, if we were in the same group, we would already know each other."

Dalia accepted his help and laughed in relief.

"Yes, really! I thought I was completely blind."

The girl adjusted the heavy glasses on her nose and smiled embarrassedly. The incident was over.

Meanwhile, quite a few passengers were left in the subway car, and it was even possible to sit in the seats.

Amir gestured for Dalia to come through and sit on the subway car bench. Dalia obediently followed his invitation, sitting down on the bench. Amir sat beside her, but they did not touch her.

"He is a real knight," Dalia thought.

Suddenly, she burst out involuntarily,

"Do you have a girlfriend?"

Amir's eyes widened. He answered.

"No..."

He hesitated but immediately continued.

"Do you have a boyfriend?"

Dalia looked away from his face, and his beautiful dark eyes lowered her eyes, and answered in a whisper,

"No."

She could think of nothing else to continue the conversation. Both sat there, staring blankly out the dark window of the subway car, in which they saw each other's reflections.

The girl had made her point, and the guy would have to take the initiative if he was interested in her. Which he did, responding.

"Let us go to the library together today. After all, we must do a term paper before the exams. It is easier to find study material and do homework that way."

Dalia, very pleased with his suggestion, replied,

"Sure! I can text you when my classes are over. Will you be at the university at 4:00 p .m.?"

He replied, glancing at his cell phone.

"Yes, I will."

His classes were ending earlier than Dalia's. Still, Amir was already determined that he would not leave this chance to get to know her better - the girl he had looked at, without tearing away, for all the lectures in the large auditorium.

Only now, he had not gone up to Dalia and got to know her, but now he would not miss his chance. This girl is a diamond! Intelligent, modest, and well-mannered. Exactly the girl he had been waiting for to find his happiness.

Amir did not know what Dalia thought of him, but he hoped that her fleeting touch on his cheek could not have been an accident, and now he had a chance, for he must have made a good impression on her. Girls of her upbringing do nothing like that without a good reason, without a real liking for a man. And because her upbringing did not allow a girl to be the first to meet guys, Amir liked that, too. He saw Dalia did not participate in their course parties and had heard nothing about her from his course friends except that she was a nerd immersed only in her studies. This was the wife he wanted to walk down the aisle, the wife he wanted to introduce to his parents, and the mother he dreamed of finding in this vast, vast metropolis.

The young couple sat on the subway car bench and looked out the opposite window.

Both were immersed in their worries, but some unknown thread bound them tightly.

Suddenly, the tunnel's darkness in the window was replaced by a stunning view of the city from the high hills of the subway stations in front of the university. The subway train jumped out of the tunnel's darkness and swiftly raced down the high trestle over the houses and gardens - like a free bird breaking free from its cage.

Below, beneath the subway overpass, the gardens flashed by. Among their foam of blooming apple and cherry trees, I could barely see the roofs of the private houses that remained in the center of the metropolis. The sky was blue, and white clouds floated leisurely across what looked like lumps of cotton candy.

Dalia and Amir looked at this beauty from the window of the subway car, rushing along the overpass as if they saw it all for the first time. However, each of them rode the subway here every day. Together, everything seemed extraordinary to them, imbued with a sense of a bright future, their bright future.

The End

ROBOTS AND LOVE

I want to tell you a love story. Or rather, two love stories. Why two? You will understand that when you read my story.

Who am I? I am a robotics engineer. My name is Serge. You would think that such a boring technician like me, always rummaging through wires and robot programs, cannot tell love stories. But you should listen to my story.

So, I work in a robotics repair center. One day, they brought me a bundle containing one robot's hard drive. It was the "brain" and "heart" of one robot device, which delivered grocery orders from the local store to customers directly to their homes. Such robots look like a bag on wheels with an antenna sensor and many "eyes" - lights and sensors in one. These robots were designed only to work as mes-

sengers - and nothing else. Their monoto-
nous work required nothing more than log-
ic in decision-making and good sensors to
navigate the walkways filled with pedestrians,
bicyclists, and electric scooters.

I accepted the repair order and set the roll
aside. It was a regular job, and I was already
bored beforehand. In the afternoon, I found
the courage to take on this tedious job of
looking for the cause of the malfunction of
the most straightforward robot messenger.
Other robot models were much more inter-
esting - for example, those that completely
mimicked pets. Or those that were made as
companions for lonely older people.

When it came to this repair order, I plugged
the hard drive into the computer and only
then looked at the fault listed by the owner
of this robot. It said the robot was constantly
deviating from the set food delivery route.
Because of this, the customers were receiving
their orders late.

I was surprised by this malfunction. If deviations from the route occur, the robot is entirely off course and drives in an unknown
direction. With the help of its tracking system,

it is possible to find it quickly and get it back on track if the cause of the malfunction is determined and the deteriorating part of its equipment is replaced. In the most "severe" cases, resetting the robot's software was possible, but this caused additional wear and tear on its sensors. We did such work only by separate agreement with the customer and at extra cost. Then the robot was good as new again.

So with Tony, a robot number thirty-eight, I was bored beforehand, not expecting anything exciting or at least profitable from this occasion, like a reboot of his entire software. But here it turned out that this robot was deviating from its set route and returning to it. Despite the delay, it delivered the order to its destination several times. It looked strange.

I looked again at the computer screen, where the dialog window with the robot software appeared, and got to work.

I typed into the dialogue window with the robot.

"I'm Serge, your repairman. What's your name?"

And immediately, I got an answer.

"I'm Tony, robot number thirty-eight. You can call me Robot Tony".

Okay, he was responding to my questions, and that was good. So the electrical impulses in his brain, his hard drive, were working.

I continued the dialogue.

"I'm investigating your deviations from the order delivery route. What do you think is the cause?"

The robots' program has a self-analysis condition. It is like self-diagnosis but at a higher level. This feature of their software helps deal with the origin of faults and saves a lot of time for diagnosis and repair.

So, in response to a simple question, I got a very extensive explanation, which I did not understand at first...

But you decide for yourself. Below is the full text of Robot Tony's explanation.

"Thank you for your inquiry about my well-being. I am not ill and find no fault in my systems. The reason for my delays on the line was Astra, robot number forty. There is no way I can miss him in my path. To shorten my explanation, I will name him Robot Astra if you do not mind.

As soon as Robot Astra comes into my field of vision, my brake system pressure rises, and I cannot move anywhere but, in the direction, directly behind that robot. Where it goes, that is where I go.

I analyzed what was happening with my systems and concluded that this malfunction was atypical.

Next, I analyzed when it all started.

I know that I first saw Robot Astra precisely twenty days ago. I use the concept of "day" as understood by programmers. My program has "a day" written on it. Still, everything is divided into a period when I have work and a rest period when I am recharging my batteries.

I have been working in the warehouse of store number fifty-one in the Central District of N. for three years. I have had only the simplest repairs and maintenance needs in all that time.

My problems with order delivery on route number fifteen began twenty days ago. I followed route number fifteen to a customer who constantly orders the same items from our store. I was not expecting any surprises along the way. Of course, there is always the possibility of some moving part in my design breaking down, so I always consider the possibility of being late on the order delivery route.

But this time, my systems were fine. Something happened when I spotted Astra, robot number forty. This robot was following ahead of me, and there was obviously something wrong with it. It could be a malfunction in his spatial orientation system. He kept stopping and turning in the opposite direction of his route, i.e., directly toward me.

I drove closer and honked my horn to give myself the way. After all, I was in a hurry to see a customer - and this is the most critical thing in my life.

Robot Astra did not give way but signaled that he needed help.

I drove closer and realized that the Robot Astra looked fine. I asked him what the problem was. Why was he not moving smoothly, as we usually move?

The Astra robot was slow to answer, so there might be other problems with its controls or sensors.

But suddenly, the Robot Astra moved closer to me and said.

"You know, I need your help exactly. They will move me out of here or scrap me if I am too late. I know how that works. And I want to be there for you so badly!"

I had no way of knowing what that meant.

"What do I mean to Robot Astra? Why does Robot Astra mean nothing to me? And what does it all mean to both of us?" I thought, and there was no way I could continue my path to my client.

So many unanswered questions began overheating my control system, and I started spinning in place.

Robot Astra was strangely looking at me. Robot Astra made some sound - like you people do when you say you are laughing. So Robot Astra did the same thing.

I could not figure out what to do now. This situation was not in my program, and I had to find a solution to the problem myself.

I stopped, turned around, and walked back to the store. I had to tell the technicians I couldn't deliver food to a customer. I needed a repair.

But the next day, I was sent back to the same customer along the same route. Once again, Robot Astra was on my path.

This time I was prepared for an unusual development of the situation. Seeing Robot Astra moving along the same route ahead of me, I slowed down. When Robot Astra blocked my path, I was about to turn around and take the alternate way I had planned for the food delivery to my customer.

It approached me, stopped, and suddenly touched my body with its antenna-sensor. I had not expected such a development. Robots rarely touch anything, much less each other. All our systems are set up to avoid touching or colliding with something or someone.

Something sparked in my hull. The momentum from the Robot Astra's touch was so strong that my sensors couldn't take it and malfunctioned. I thought I saw sparks in my eyes from the electrical discharge.

But nothing happened. I ran a self-test, and the program reported nothing wrong with my systems.

What was it? What was it I was seeing and feeling?

Robot Astra was staring at me, and its sensor antennas were frozen, waiting for my next move. I did not know what to do, but I decided that next time I would consider this effect of the robot Astra's touch and ask for better protection against the static electricity generated in the external environment.

Nothing else happened. Robot Astra stood like that for a while, wiggled its sensor antennas, and went on again. We did not exchange a word this time. Just that electric shock...

We drove away with the Astra robot in different directions, and I was once again late for my customer, as I had taken a detour to ensure the safe delivery of my order.

The next day, I did not have to take that route and completed all my orders immediately.

A week went by. I did not see Robot Astra on the other routes. I kept getting ready to meet Robot Astra, which was not on my route. Something was causing me tension as if I was missing something. Maybe my battery was dead.

Yesterday I saw Robot Astra again. It was loaded into the back of a truck, ready to be sent to the robotics landfill. Robot Astra number forty was finally out of commission, as he suggested.

However, when this truck with the robots being sent to the junkyard drove by me, I felt a faint prick-impulse, as if something had touched my body again. But there was no one around. And there was no way Robot Astra could have touched me from there - five meters between us.

When the robot truck, entirely out of commission, was completely ready to leave our warehouse grounds, just as I caught a faint sound as if someone was calling my name.

I looked around but saw no one.

Suddenly, one antenna of the Robot Astra lying in the back of the truck lifted. I realized there was still a charge in its battery.

A wave of energy lifted me like a current had penetrated my body and swirled through my wires.

I approached the truck and turned to its driver—thankfully, he was human.

"Dear fellow, could you help me find my way out of this warehouse? It is my first time here."

What was that? Was I not telling the truth? Was it according to the program? If it was a program, who wrote it? I did not know that; I just used this opportunity to communicate with the person and tell him what I wanted to say. Even if it was not true. I was giving the information I needed so the truck driver would get out of the car, and the shipment would be slightly delayed.

Indeed, the truck driver got out of the truck's cab and considered the gate from which I could get out of the warehouse and go to the customer with the order.

Meanwhile, I drove closer to the truck and told the Robot Astra.

"If you can, get out of there. I distracted the driver."

Robot Astra replied in a faint voice.

"I will try. I hope there is enough battery for that."

He pushed the hulls of the stationary robots around him, clearly out of his last strength, got up, leaned his pincer arms on the truck bed floor, and fell from there straight to the ground, hitting his body hard.

I drove closer to Robot Astra and inspected its damage, gently probing its hull with my sensor antennas. The body of Robot Astra number forty was severely dented, but my diagnostics showed that it was otherwise fine.

I asked,

"Well, can you move on? We have got to find a place to hide."

Robot Astra answered me.

"Yes, I can still move for a while. But my charge is ending..."

I spun on the spot, looking around, and saw no one at our working robot charging rack.

We drove up there and stood on charge. While our batteries were charging, we did not talk. Robot Astra occasionally touched my body with its sensor antenna, and I responded by touching it with my antenna. We did not need to speak, but our plans were already evident. When we were both 100% charged, we looked at each other, still not saying a word. We drove away from that work robot yard - into the street, then further and further along the route we knew - towards the customer's house on route number fifteen.

We drove through many intersections before the tracking services found us.

We were separated. I was sent for repairs and research. I am still trying to figure out what happened to Robot Astra. I think he was taken to the junkyard. And I will not be able to help it anymore. However, I do not rule out the possibility that Robot Astra could get away again. When the repair workers took him into their pickup truck, his battery was still charged. He might get away again and find me.

I am realistic about my perspective - as the instigator of our departure from the robot yard, I am more likely to be written off to the scrap yard. My program is not working; I am doing actions not designed for."

Robot Tony, number thirty-eight, gave me this information, and his dialogue window went out.

I could not understand why I considered Robot Tony, number thirty-eight, an individual. It could not be! Everything he told me seemed unbelievable. It was just some programmer who had written this program to amuse himself and make fun of me. I would find out who it was and show him where the crayfish were.

At that moment, a hand rested on my shoulder, and a melodious female voice was heard behind me.

"Well, have you figured out his malfunction? The whole department is already wondering if you can cope with this repair. They gave it to us first, but we could not determine the cause of its malfunction."

Behind me was my colleague, Svetlana. She occasionally stopped by to chat and have coffee with me.

I turned to her and replied.

"I do not know what is wrong with this robot, but all together - his story and his reactions - it seems like..."

"...love," Svetlana continued my line.

"Yes, it sounds like love."

I turned fully around in my chair and noted for the umpteenth time how beautiful she was-a slender figure, long blond hair braided into a thick braid, and huge gray eyes.

But I would never dare ask her to even go to a cafe, let alone on a date with me. I'm such an ordinary guy, and she's just a beauty...

I was embarrassed and, lowering my gaze, muttered,

"Robots cannot feel. When it says 'feel,' it means 'feel' with sensors. A robot cannot love..."

Svetlana crossed her arms over her chest and rested her hip on the edge of my desk.

"They cannot? Sometimes I think some people are much more robotic than our subjects."

There was both sadness and sarcasm in her voice at the same time.

I initially wanted to reply, but when I met her gaze, I suddenly realized she meant me.

"I..." I mumbled, frantically searching for words. "Am I so insensitive? But what am I supposed to do if..."

Svetlana stepped away from my desk and, already standing at the door of my room, answered,

"You are just a monster compared to this ro-bot. You do not notice anything around you. You do not notice anyone around you..."

She left, shutting the door quietly.

I sat there, staring blankly at the screen with the text of Robot Tony's explanation.

Had I offended her by not noticing some-thing? Svetlana is so attractive. I never thought about the fact that she might like me. I am a complete introvert and never dare to tell myself how much I like her.

I jumped up from my seat and ran down the corridor after Svetlana. She, hearing my foot-steps, turned around in surprise and, seeing my expression, smiled gently as if she had been waiting for me to do just that.

I ran up to Svetlana, stopped at arm's length from her, and tried to catch my breath to find the words to tell her how much I had wanted to tell her how much I liked her. I wanted to finally tell her how much I wanted to touch her face, her lips. I wanted to tell her she was the most beautiful person in the world.

But Svetlana beat me to it. She touched my chest lightly with her hand, and then suddenly, she was so close to me that I had no choice but to embrace her.

I buried my face in her thick, soft hair and felt the vein in her neck beat. Svetlana pressed harder against me, wrapped her arms around my waist with both hands, and kissed me first on the cheek and then right on the lips. Our breath became one breath; our bodies became one body. Our hearts became one heart.

A month later, Svetlana and I became husband and wife. We bought a house with a large lot, and our dogs and parrot also took up residence there. At our housewarming party, our entire robot repair department was walking around, and it was hilarious to see that our wedding was a big surprise for most of their colleagues. No one expected such a beautiful woman as Svetlana could find something special in an inconspicuous guy like me. But, as she told me, looks do not determine the essence of a person. My future wife saw something in me that attracted her more than the pumped-up muscles of other guys.

But our main housewarming party was the four of us - because in our garage, we made room for two completely useless creatures or mechanisms in our household. The robots named Tony, number thirty-eight, and Astra, number forty, had a housewarming party with us.

Before we bought the house, Svetlana and I bought them from a grocery delivery company. I reprogrammed them so they no longer cared about the delivery routes to customers but more about the weather and whether to cut the grass. Of course, the grass mower was also a robot, and it was their pet they took care of. Or was it more than a pet to them? We do not know that.

And another thing: Svetlana and I did not touch the part of the program responsible for their unusual affection for each other. We will never know who made such a joke about these robots, but they and their example gave us the impetus to think about who we need around us. So now our robotic romantics could communicate and call each other simply by name, without a number. We can give our gift to them for the beginning of their lives together. Why? It was not just me and Svetlana to be happy!

The End

CYNTHIA AND THE OLD HOTEL

Cynthia looked at the building of a little old hotel in the foothills of a famous resort town at a loss.

She inherited it from a distant relative and could not understand why she had not disinherited it immediately. And now she had to estimate the work to restore the hotel before it could be sold. However, no one had thought to leave her any money for that.

But Cynthia was open and went to the bank to get a loan. To do this, she had to take over the firm's management that handled the hotel's business. The firm had very few employees-just her, Cynthia.

But today, a restoration contractor would finally come to her and advise her on what to do here and how to do it.

Cynthia heard a car pulling up and turned around.

A stout man in his early thirties stepped out of a tattered pickup truck that had stopped in the circle in front of the hotel's main entrance. He was dressed in a construction worker's uniform. In the thirty-degree Celsius heat, he wore no shirt, and the straps of his blue work overalls stressed the man's muscular, tanned arms and broad shoulders.

The construction worker, squinting slightly, hesitated a little at his car, then decided and walked over to Cynthia and said,

"Good afternoon. Are you Cynthia?"

Cynthia replied.

"Yes, I am. And you are George, I believe?"

"Yes," he replied, holding his hand for a handshake.

Cynthia shook his hand briefly. In doing so, she thought he held her hand in his a little, but it was only for a moment. Or did she want him to have her hand in his?

After three years of divorce from her husband, Cynthia seemed determined to forget everything to do with men and was immersed in her work. And now all her attention was concentrated on the restoration of this hotel, which appeared so untimely in her life.

The young woman was only twenty-six years old, so she did not think she needed to rush into choosing her next life partner.

Cynthia walked George around the hotel. The man walked around the old building and did not frighten Cynthia with the substantial renovation costs. He was ticking off a questionnaire about what needed to be done.

When they finished making their rounds of the hotel, George said.

"I will send you a cost estimate in a couple of days. I have your company contacts, so wait for the data. I hope they will be within your means. However, you always have the option of doing a cost estimate with other contractors - and choosing the most appropriate estimate and firm."

"Thanks for the information, but let's start with you," Cynthia replied with a polite smile. She had already received several estimates and had yet to tell the following contractor.

A couple of days later, Cynthia received cost estimates from George's firm, which were the most reasonable from her point of view. One thing was a risk factor - George was the only employee at his firm, and that meant that if he did not continue the work himself, all plans to rebuild the hotel as quickly as possible might be in jeopardy, as well as the timing of her payments on the hotel renovation loan.

But Cynthia decided she would take that risk and control everything George did at the hotel. Fortunately, she had time for that now-she quit her job and devoted all her time to this hotel.

Cynthia rented a cabin near the hotel and came to the hotel every day like she was going to work. Yes, her new job was renovating and selling the hotel. The place was good for tourists, so Cynthia expected to make good money when she sold the hotel.

The lodge was about three hundred feet from the building. Cynthia was comfortable coming to the hotel every morning, leaving it only for lunch and then going home.

The old hotel gradually drew Cynthia in more. As if magnetically drawn, she was increasingly fond of the walls, aged and unpainted, and the windows that gave a view of the once lavish and well-tended garden.

In the garden's center was a small artificial pond with a fountain. Cynthia had not budgeted to restore this pond and green, so she did it herself. Every day she tidied up the garden around the fountain pool little by little, and she also filled the fountain with water and put goldfish in it. She began her day by going to the hotel and feeding the goldfish, who came to the pool's edge as soon as they spotted her.

George showed up at the hotel every workday. He took Cynthia through the repairs to the hotel and its facilities. Cynthia was so used to him talking to her every day in his calm, husky voice one time when George did not show up at the hotel at the usual start time of work. She became nervous. Cynthia was not thinking about him quitting project no. She thought only of what had happened to him.

And something had happened to him. George had been in a car accident and was confined to a hospital bed.

When Cynthia found out he was in the hospital, she dropped everything and went to see him. In the emergency room, a woman told her she was a colleague of George's. The nurse looked at her slyly and said.

"Yes, of course." But you could see from her face that she did not believe Cynthia.

Cynthia walked to the room where George lay.

When she entered his room, George was speechless. His right arm was in a sling, a bandage running from it across his chest. He was shirtless - because even here, it was so hot. But Cynthia was now used to seeing him shirtless and sat in the chair beside his bed.

George was surprised. He tried to get up on the bed and sat higher, resting his back on the pillows.

Cynthia said,

"Well, there, I found you."

They had switched to "you" some time ago when Cynthia realized she was spending more time with George than anyone else in her entourage.

The young woman took a couple of chocolates from her bag and a bottle of natural juice she had made from berries in her hotel garden and placed it all on the nightstand by George's bedside. He watched her actions with amazement.

"You seem to have taken over for me?" he said with a smile and moved closer to Cynthia.

Leaning toward her, he continued in a conspiratorial tone,

"And what did you say to the medical sisters that they let you through to me?"

Cynthia laughed and, pleased with her adventure, replied.

"That I was your friend."

She did not know why she lied to him. Perhaps she wanted to embarrass him even more-he looked so funny when he was embarrassed. Usually so sure of himself, George looked like a boy when he was sorry. And she liked that very much.

They talked some more about George's well-being, and Cynthia left. She was left with a warm feeling about how they spoke to George. Usually, he was quiet and focused on his hotel repair business and did not claim Cynthia's time or her attention.

Now Cynthia felt she cared more, not about the hotel being idle. She waited for the repairs to be completed, but about George being there for her as soon as possible.

But Cynthia tempered these feelings by sometimes reprimanding herself aloud,

"That is just what you want. He is just working around, that is all."

George spent only a few days in the hospital and was discharged home. Fortunately, his injuries were minor, and he could continue working after a week. His right hand worked, although he had to do a lot with his left hand, which slowed him down considerably.

Cynthia did not ask George when he would finish the hotel renovation work. She did not want him out of her life. And she did not know how to tell him that.

Cynthia did not even know if he was marrie d... She and George did not talk about any- thing like that. I just wanted to let you know that there was no need to. But Cynthia felt a growing need in her soul to see him around, to know that she could rely on him, on his calmness, his confidence in what and how he was doing, and she also liked the fact that he was running his firm alone-just as she had run her - temporarily her - hotel business.

When the renovation work on the hotel was almost finished, the locals in the village next to the hotel threw a big party. In the evening, Cynthia came to the party only to admire the fireworks and taste the local Highlanders' dishes, which were simply amazing.

Cynthia walked out into the square of the small mountain village, decorated with brightly colored garlands, and looked around. She did not know anyone there, but local women immediately called her over and treated her to their homemade sweets and drinks.

Cynthia sat on a boardwalk under a canopy decorated with garlands of colorful lights and surveyed the square. A local orchestra played in the yard, and couples danced to cheerful music.

Suddenly, Cynthia recognized George as the man dancing on the platform in the center of the square. Her heart raced as if she were running somewhere. She should have fled from here for. He was dancing with someone else!

Cynthia watched George dance deftly with the other woman, and her mind noted with unknown pain how she looked at her partner. That woman was thrilled to be dancing with George, which burned Cynthia's heart like fire.

Cynthia turned away, trying to cope with her feelings. The music became a quiet melody, and the romantically inclined couple twirled under the starry sky in a slow dance.

Cynthia got up to leave this celebration, which had become torture. She did not want to be here anymore. True, she still could not fathom that George dancing here with another woman had so ruined her mood.

Cynthia put her sweatshirt in her bag, and no sooner had she stepped away from the bench than George's voice rang out nearby.

"Aha, there you are!" he said, walking toward her.

He stopped right in front of Cynthia. His plaid shirt was unbuttoned, and he continued when he saw Cynthia's gaze resting on his chest, on which a gold chain with some symbol on a pendant, the sign of his Zodiac, gleamed.

"So, shall we go dancing?"

Cynthia could not believe her ears. Was he asking her to dance? Him? But he had just been dancing so enthusiastically with that other woman...

George stared at Cynthia, waiting for her answer. He had already had time to catch his breath, and his voice was again with that huskiness so familiar to her.

Cynthia replied.

"All right... I only have to put my things some-where. I was not going to..."

"To dance?" interjected George. He guessed her words and her thoughts. "But here you and I are going dancing, and you can count on me-no one here will touch your things. Even leave your purse on this bench. Believe me, there are only locals here and no thieves among them."

Cynthia was embarrassed by her suspicions. But she was even more embarrassed that now she had to feel his hands, so strong and familiar to her from her work at the hotel, touching her body.

It was as if George understood her confusion and said,

"Come, come! Here comes a fun song, just right for you and me."

Cynthia realized he wanted to dance a dance with her that required a little touching from each other.

And in her heart, she was grateful to him for that. She would have been a little uncomfortable if right there, right away, she had to feel his touch and heated body next to hers.

They walked to the dance floor, and George gallantly offered his hand to Cynthia as she stepped onto the platform.

The music was fast, and Cynthia was drawn to this unpretentious dance. Their couple moved well to the rhythm of the dance.

A hyped-up Cynthia and George stopped on the platform when the music stopped. Cynthia realized she had to decide whether to continue dancing if the music changed to a slow tune. But no sooner had Cynthia decided anything than she felt George's arms gently encircle her waist and draw her closer to his body. The young woman at first rested her hands on his chest, just out of surprise. But then she realized it was just a dance and surrendered herself to her dance partner. George skillfully led her to a slow dance where she did not have to do anything but follow his movements.

Cynthia said nothing. She did not have to say anything to feel his breath on her face him-just, feel his body through her sweat-soaked shirt, and know that she wanted this dance to go on and on.

But all good things always end sometime. The music died down, and the other pairs of dancers left the platform. The musicians had taken a break, or the concert was over.

Cynthia and George were still hugging each other on the platform, unable to keep their hands off each other. An unknown force drew them in, preventing them from breaking the circle of their arms and bodies.

Cynthia lifted her face and looked George in the eyes. She realized - he was looking at her with such admiration that no words were necessary. The taciturn George could have said nothing more to her-just hugged her like he was doing now.

George tilted his head slightly toward Cynthia's face and said.

"Well, it is all over now..."

He did not let Cynthia out of his embrace. He waited to see what she would say or do.

Cynthia replied.

"Yes, it is over..."

Nor did she make any attempt to free herself from his embrace.

George ran his hand down Cynthia's back from her waist to her shoulders, hugged the woman gently, and pulled her to his chest.

"You do not have to say anything. Cynthia, I..."

Cynthia did not think to say anything. She felt the heat of his body with her whole body. She needed that security of his arms so badly. The vibration of his voice echoed in her chest as the playing of a classical guitar resonated with our hearts.

The couple stood like that without saying another word.

Everything that awaited them in the future was clear by now. Long-contained feelings rushed out through the doors of their souls, suddenly opened by the music, the whiff of the warm summer wind in the night, and the endless starry sky above the lovers' heads.

The End

Copyright by Misha Quinn, June 2023

Please, be so kind as to leave a good review and rate by stars ** my stories in this online bookstore and on Goodreads. Thank you!**
*****

I like to write easy-to-read short stories with short paragraphs, clean or sweet, with some instalove and feel-good atmosphere of each standalone, flash-fiction romantic story.
If you want to know more about romance novels written by Misha Quinn, please, look at Misha's website:
http://www.mishaquinn.com/
You will find links to ebooks, paperbacks, large print paperback editions, and audiobooks.
With best regards, Misha Quinn, writer

BONUS CONTENT FOR YOU

Get the FREE bonus prologue to the 2nd book in The Salamander series when you sign up for my newsletter:

http://www.mishaquinn.com/

Please subscribe to the newsletter and download Misha Quinn bonus content.

Sincerely yours, Misha Quinn

Also by Misha Quinn

You can find all of Misha's books and other information on the author's website:

http://www.mishaquinn.com

EBOOKS & PAPERBACKS & LARGE PRINT PA-PERBACKS & AUDIOBOOKS

The Heart of a Salamander – A Fae Fantasy Romance Series

The Salamander - A Billionaire Boss Romance Series

Sunset Lake Club - A Sweet Later-in-life Romance Series

Sunset Lake Club LARGE PRINT Novels Editions – A Sweet Later-in-life Romance Series

Romance Short Story Collections: A Heart-warming, Feel-Good, Easy-Read Fiction Series – with LARGE PRINT paperback editions

MY DEAR READER,

As a self-published author, I make every effort to ensure readers enjoy my books. As of this book's publication date, I do everything myself- create and write my story, covers, proofread, edit, read again, etc.

If you have any comments or suggestions about the quality of the text in this or another of my books, for example, about a phrase or word that needs to be corrected to make it sound better in context, please write your suggestions directly to me, via the contact form on the author's website:

http://www.mishaquinn.com/contact/

Thank you in advance for your help!

Sincerely, Misha Quinn, writer

About the Author

Misha Quinn is a pen name of an independently published contemporary & fantasy romance author from Finland, with over 20 novels, novellas, and short stories published. With Misha's wide life experience, love of practical psychology, and knowing both the creative arts and business world, she likes to create romantic stories with a pinch of adventures, suspense, and paranormal events. Misha's heroines are mostly strong women, or they get stronger during their life lessons.

Author's website> http://www.mishaquinn.com/

Milton Keynes UK
Ingram Content Group UK Ltd.
UKHW020657231023
431165UK00015B/665